"In the district of Titicaca, once there lived Macaca
Scruffy old Macaca with a bristle on her tail."

Welcome to the district of Titicaca, an exotic lake, situated
between Peru and Bolivia inhabited by local animals and
migrants from surrounding terrains. You will be following
an exciting adventure of a Brazilian student, Macaca, who
became a real heroine amongst Titicaca's population due
to her strong spirit and inventive mind.

To order additional copies of this book, contact:
Xlibris
0800-056-3182
www.xlibrispublishing.co.uk
Orders@ Xlibrispublishing.co.uk

# Adventure of Brave Macaca

## Nataliya Blanchard

Illustrations by
**Nicola Lecciones**

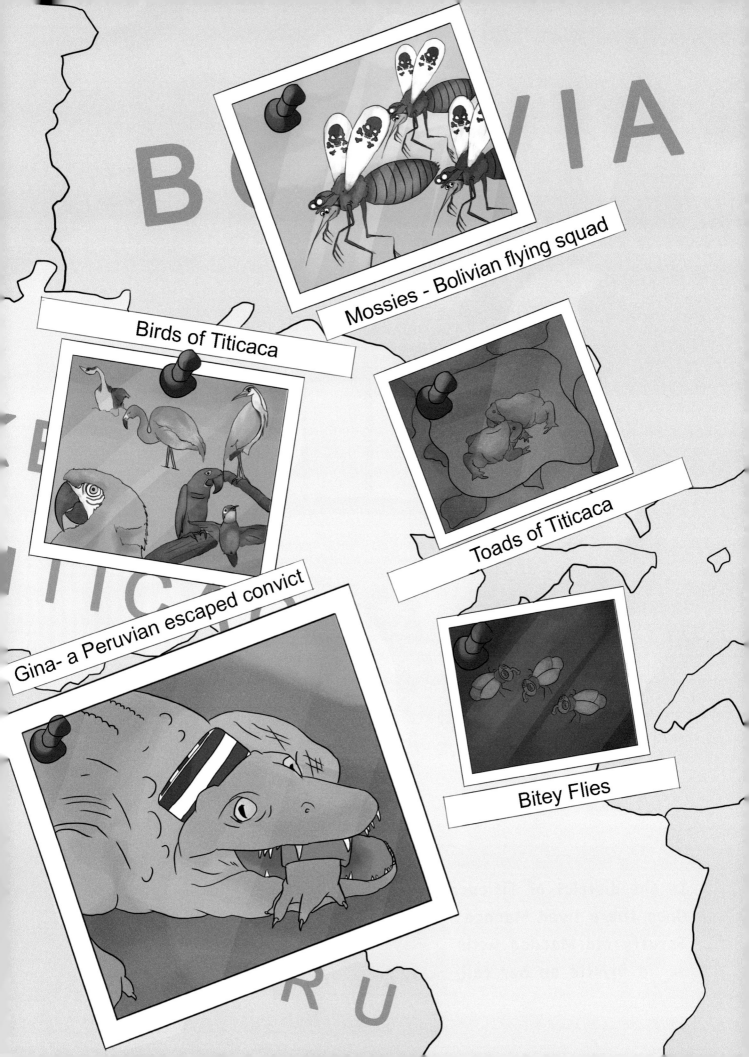

Mossies - Bolivian flying squad

Birds of Titicaca

Toads of Titicaca

Gina- a Peruvian escaped convict

Bitey Flies

In the district of Titicaca
Once there lived Macaca
Scruffy old Macaca with
a bristle on her tail

WELCOME

All beasts of Titicaca
All birds of Titicaca
All toads of Titicaca
And even Hippo po
Loved, cherished and
    welcomed that Macaca
Scruffy old Macaca with
    a bristle on her tail

Once in waters of Titicaca
In the darkness of a bog
A Crocodile called Gina emerged

This green and cunning monster
Used to trick his victims
Pretending to be asleep
And then he gobbled up
   the poor creatures
What a disgusting creep!

Brave scruffy old Macaca
    with a bristle on her tail
Went out on a mission
To lure the nasty villain
Into an iron cage

But wise and brave Macaca
Drew perfect noughts and crosses
Tickling the tongue of the
cunning monster
With a bristle on her tail

Exhausted but still proud Gina
Burped out this irritating grief
And mumbled with relief:
"Well, then, you live, Macaca,
Scruffy old Macaca with
    a bristle on your tail

I won't chase you any longer
But to survive and not to drown from hunger
From now on I'll follow a healthy diet of
Tasty bitey flies in reasonable doses
And even malaria-carrying mossies!"

Since then in the district
of Titicaca
Happily lived Macaca
Scruffy old Macaca with
a bristle on her tail

# Cast:

Macaca
Crocodile
Hippopotamus (Hippo po)
Anaconda
Sloth

## Beasts of Titicaca:
Andean Wolf
Andean Fox
Llama
Vizcacha
Skunk

Wild Guinea Pig

## Birds of Titicaca:
Grebe
Chilian Pink Flamingo
Blue Heron
Macaw
Parrot

Humming Bird

## Toads of Titicaca:
Giant Titicaca Frogs

## Bitey Flies:
Fat Green Flies

## Bolivian flying squad:
Mosquitos (Mossies)

Printed in the United States
By Bookmasters